Krampus's

Great Big Book

of

Yuletide Monsters

For Toby,
on your first Christmas

Krampus's
Great Big Book
of
Yuletide Monsters

Poems and Doodles by
Amanda R. Woomer
As Told to by
Krampus

Frohe Weinchten, children.

It's the most frightful time of year.

The season of monsters and darkness

Not just merriment and cheer.

These winter days are cold and short

As the dark of night becomes longer.

You can sense that mischief is afoot

The Yuletide monsters grow stronger.

If you've been good all year long

You have nothing to fear,

For Father Nicholas

Soon will be here.

But if you've been naughty—

You have much to dread.

My monsters are hungry.

And they demand to be fed.

You will not find gifts

On that bright Christmas morn,

For from these beasts

Nightmares are born.

So follow me, brave children!

That is if you dare.

Meet my Christmas monsters

And see how you'll fare.

La Befana

I don't want to frighten you

Since we've only just begun.

Meet Italy's Christmas Witch

Who likes to visit everyone.

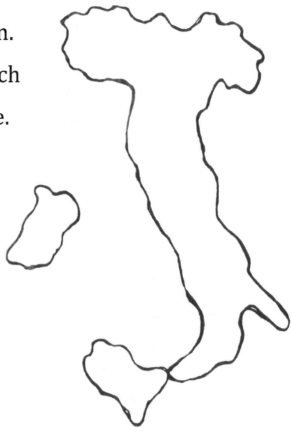

She comes down your chimney

Like someone else you know.

And if you've been good

Small gifts she'll bestow.

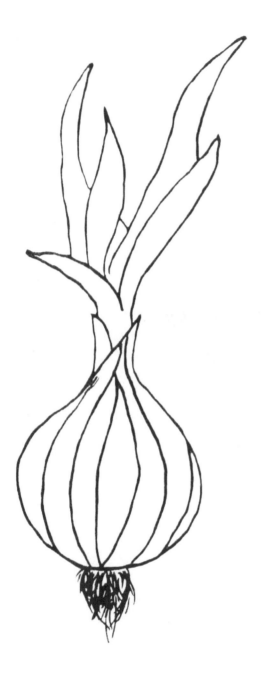

But to the wicked ones,

She gives an onion and coal.

It could be much worse—

She could devour your soul.

Leave out some wine

And you'll have nothing to dread.

But if you see the witch,

She'll hit you on the head.

This Christmas Witch

Is not nearly as frightful

As the next creature we'll meet

Who is just a tad bit spiteful.

Tomtar

Let's journey a bit further

To the Scandinavian north,

Home to the *nisse* and *tontuu*—

Known as Tomtar henceforth.

Little round men

With a knit cap and beard.

But don't let looks fool you,

These things should be feared.

They hide in the burial mounds,

Living among the dead.

When they arrive on your doorstep,

Carefully you must tread.

Work hard at your chores.

Keep your home nice and clean.

If you heed what they ask,

They will never be mean.

Help them out of the way

If something should fall.

Don't undo their hard work,

For they hate that most of all.

But if you don't listen

And don't heed my warning,

Your mother and father

Might find themselves mourning.

Tomtar can be wicked!

They're known for their bite!

Anyone they dislike

Their poison will smite.

Leave them a small present

This next Christmas Eve.

Porridge with butter's

Their favorite, I believe.

Knecht Ruprecht

Farmhand Rupert was once

A small child just like you—

Feral and wild—

You don't believe me? It's true!

He now follows St. Nicholas

All over the land

With a bag full of ashes

And a staff in his hand.

Apples and gingerbread

For those who do pray.

But if not, my poor child,

Trouble comes your way.

I do hope you're fast!

You'd better go hide!

He'll whack you with his sack

And those ashes inside!

But that is not all—

Did you find a stick in your shoe?

That's Knecht Ruprecht's gift

To your parents, not you.

So be sure you behave,

And do say your prayer.

If not, on St. Nick's Day

Ruprecht will be there.

Frau Perchta

The Bright One was a goddess

In days long gone by.

But today she's a witch,

On a broom she does fly.

Over a thousand years old,

She judges all from her broom.

And if you displease her,

She'll sneak into your room.

With rocks and with straw,

She'll stuff you quite full.

Unless you've eaten her favorite

A meal of fish and of gruel.

If she likes you she'll leave

A silver coin in your shoe.

To avoid a belly of straw,

Here's what to do:

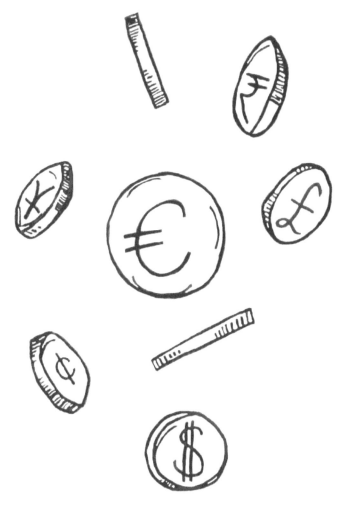

Offer Frau Perchta

Food and drink at your door.

As she flies on her broom,

She'll give good luck galore.

Karakoncolos

You've heard of a devil

And a Sasquatch, I'm sure!

Now let's head to Turkey

On this holiday tour.

It's home to a beast

Tall, hairy, and brown.

And if you're not careful

You'll find him 'bout town.

Mr. Karakoncolos

Is a fan of riddles, you see.

To survive your encounter

You must answer wisely.

No matter the question

In his verbal attack,

Your answer must always

Include the word "black."

Lucky for you,

He's not always around.

In the heart of winter

These beasts are found.

For only ten days

They're allowed to roam.

But if you're not careful,

They'll lure you from home.

Sounding just like your parents

They'll cry from the snow.

But if you are wise

You'll stay put and not go.

What a frightful creature

This Karakoncolos,

Whose path please be sure

You never do cross.

But the things they hate most

I'll kindly tell you:

They hate basil and ivy

To name just a few.

So if you find yourself wandering

On a cold *Zemheri* night,

Answer simply with "black"

And then run out of sight.

Mari Lwyd

For some, it's a reindeer—

The symbol of the day,

But in Wales there's a creature

That likes to say neigh.

If you said it's a horse

Well, you're almost right,

But little Mari Lwyd

Is a bit of a sight.

With ribbons and bells

On a horse's skull,

This wassailing tradition

Is anything but dull.

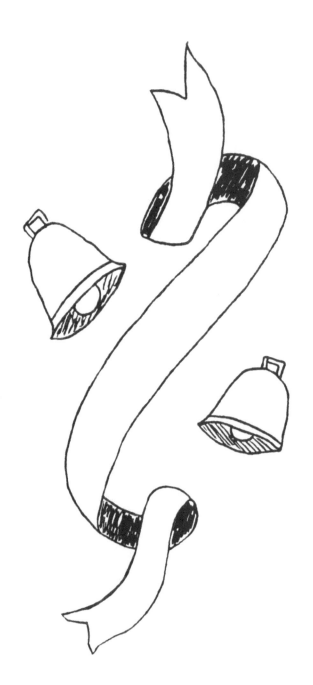

The revelers and dancers

Wander from home to home.

For food and for drink

Through the whole town they roam.

They'll offer a song

In exchange for food.

To keep them out

Sing twice as good

So don't be surprised

And don't be rude!

Invite her inside

When you meet Mari Lwyd.

Sack Man

Now some might cry out:

"Not another Knecht Ruprecht!"

But he is far worse

Than most would expect.

This bogeyman is found

All over the globe,

Carrying his sack

And wearing a robe.

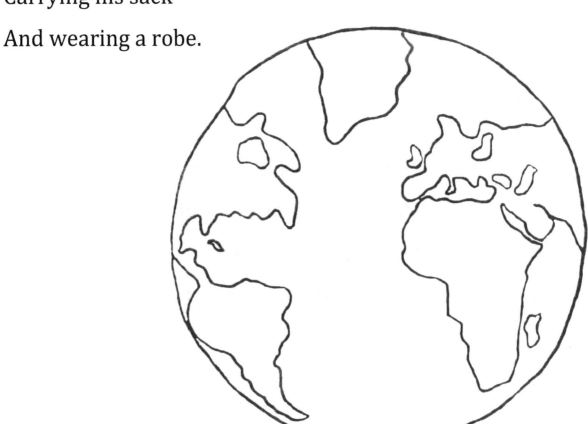

He's Tonton Macoute

In the language of Haitian,

And Abu I Kees

In the Lebanon nation.

He's called Babaroga

In lands throughout Europe,

And the Karqyt of Turkey

Doesn't offer much hope.

The Sack Man is everywhere—
Vietnam and in Spain.
There's nowhere to run
It would just be in vain!

The Sack Man will know
If you're naughty or nice.
To avoid this old monster
Heed my advice:

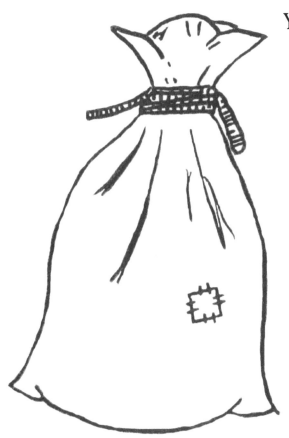

He'll drag you from home,

Tie you up in his sack!

And no matter your tears

You'll never come back!

For he'll drag you to Hell!

To the depths of despair!

And your mommy and daddy

Will ne'er find you there.

So be extra good,

And be sure you behave...

For fear that you may

Be dragged to your grave .

Gryla, the Yule Lads, and their Yule Cat

Iceland's most frightful family

To me, it would seem,

Finds pleasure in making

The countryside scream.

The family is led

By a fierce giantess.

They roam lava fields.

Why, is anyone's guess.

Grýla is her name,

O'er three hundred years old.

She likes to eat children,

Or so I am told.

She watches them play

All throughout the year,

And when winter arrives,

That's when she draws near.

She steals all the children,

Brings them back to her cave.

And suddenly they wish

That they would have behaved.

Grýla's cauldron is bubbling

As her tummy does rumble.

And into the pot

Each child does tumble.

Grýla eats them all up.

How she does love her stew!

Sometimes with her sons

She will share her brew.

They're known as the Yule Lads—

Thirteen in all.

How they'll play tricks on you

As the dark night does fall.

There's Stubby and Meat-Hook,

And old *Askasleikir*.

Don't forget *Þvörusleiker*,

That nasty Spoon-Licker.

If you've been good all year long,

A gift they might leave.

But a potato the wicked

Might just receive.

A visit from them

Might not be that scary.

But they're joined by a creature

That is far more hairy.

The *Jólakötturinn*

Is a fearsome beast!

And if you're not careful

You'll be her next feast!

She prowls the countryside,

This wicked Yule Cat,

Looking for anyone

Without a new hat.

For that's how you save

Your life and your soul,

Or your punishment is something

Far worse than just coal.

Buy yourself new clothes

Before Christmas Eve night,

Or else that old Yule Cat

Will give you a fright.

Iceland's own ancient family

Is a grisly old sight,

So please heed my warning

On this Christmas night:

Be good all year round,

And get some new clothes.

After that, all that's left

Is to pray, I suppose.

Belsnickel

Now let's journey to America

For this next Christmas gent.

He's found in Pennsylvania

Among the Deutsch descent.

He's a grumpy old man,

All clad in his furs.

And just a week before Yule,

He visits young boys and girls.

With a switch in his hand,

The naughty he beats.

But inside his pockets

Are cakes, nuts, and sweets.

The fur-clad old man

Is a sight to behold.

One that might bring you joy

If you do what you're told.

He'll knock on your door

On a dark winter night.

Greet him with song

And be sure you're polite.

He'll offer you candy –

Just don't ask for more!

The Belsnickel might hit you

And walk out the door.

Kallikantzaros

Feral cats and dead horses

Strange stories to hear,

But there's a beast down in Greece

To make you tremble in fear.

They're small and they're ugly,

They live underground.

Tis but once a year

They're allowed to come 'round.

They spend their days sawing

At the ancient world tree,

But as the days grow short

They are finally free.

The twelve days of Christmas—
It's a frightening time—
When the Kallikantzaros
Begin their climb.

They creep into homes,
Could already be here!
And if you're not careful,
These nasties draw near.

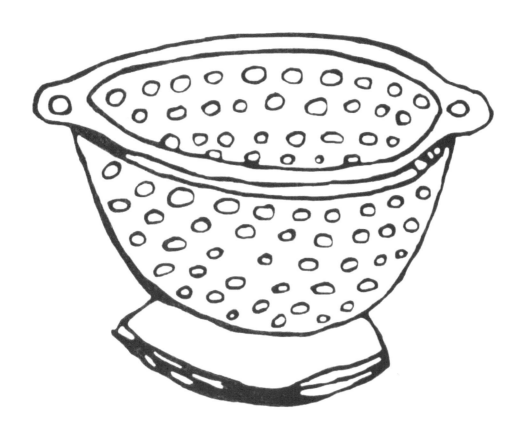

Safe homes will have

Colanders at the door.

For these evil sprites

Cannot count to four.

Or into the fire,

Toss your old smelly shoes.

They can't stand the smell!

Your house they won't choose.

Kallikantzaros are wicked!

They're nasty old beasts!

They'll only cause mischief

Til Epiphany's Feast.

Then it's back underground

To finish their job.

Though each year I think

I hear a small sob.

For *Moriai* is alive!

The World Tree still stands!

You see, the Kallikantzaros

Just don't understand.

While they're up above

Causing mischief and pain,

The World Tree is healing.

It just drives them insane!

They go straight back to work,

And begin once again.

They twist and they hurry,

Their backs in a strain.

But as the snow falls,

It begins once more.

The Kallikantzaros leave *Moriai*

And come knock on your door.

Lussi

Perhaps you've heard of St. Lucia,

Full of love and of light.

But the eve of her feast

Is Lussi's Long Night.

December thirteenth

Was once so long ago,

The dark Winter Solstice

When the cold wind would blow.

Lucia's bright candles

On top of her head,

Would remind the wealthy

They had nothing to dread.

But the eve of her feast—

The twelfth of December—

Was the night simple folk

Would always remember.

Throughout the town

On her broom she would fly:

Lussi and her demons,

Known as *Oskorei*.

It's a wild hunt,

With monsters and trolls.

And Lussi would sometimes

Raise long lost dead souls.

She'll come down your chimney

If your work is not done.

So make sure you leave her

A hot saffron bun.

Don't venture outside,

Lest you be dragged away

To the skies with the monsters

Amidst all the fray.

It's best to stay home

Far from worry and strife.

Scissors over the door

Might just save your life.

Keep a fire going,

Fill your home with its light.

A *Lussevaka* they say

Should stay up all night.

For if you've done well,

And your house is all clean,

Lussi flies by

She'll never be seen.

As the sun slowly sets

On the eve of the twelfth,

Say thanks to Old Lussi

For your life and your health.

She's let you go on,

There is nothing to fear.

She will keep her demons

From drawing too near.

For Lussi and Lucia

Are one and the same.

Their light shines through winter.

For that's both their name.

Krampus

We've traveled the world

From Haiti to Turkey,

But there's one monster left—

That's right, it is me!

For I'm the baddest of them all!

I'm certainly no saint!

And when I come to town,

I'm sure you'll grow faint.

I'm older by far

Than Christmas itself.

I've been around longer than

That jolly old elf.

I'm covered in fur,

With horns and with hooves.

At the sight of my *Ruten*,

Your behavior improves.

I rattle my chains

And make room in my sack.

We are Hell bound, you see!

There is no coming back.

Saint Nicholas comes

On December the sixth.

But tis the night before

That I play my tricks.

So be sure that you're good

If you don't wish to see me.

For come *Krampusnacht*,

There'll be nowhere to flee.

There you have it, dear child!

Twelve monsters for you.

Now let us look back,

And count in review:

La Befana's a witch

Who rides on her broom.

The Tomtar, they like

To live in a tomb.

Knecht Ruprecht he's known

To hit you with ashes.

Frau Perchta will stuff you

And leave you with gashes.

Karakoncolos's answer

Must always be black.

Mari Lwyd just wants to

Come in for a snack.

The Sack Man is found

All over the globe.

And Grýla's Yule Cat

Must see your new robe.

The Belsnickel is grumpy,

And ugly, and old.

Kallikantzaros just want

The world to unfold.

Down your chimney comes Lussi

If your work is not done.

And I drag some to Hell

Just for fun.

We're not here to hurt you.

Oh believe me, my child!

We're here to remind you

That winter is wild!

The days have grown short.

It's dark and it's cold.

But keep yourself warm

With these stories I've told.

They're older than Christmas,

Perhaps even Yule!

If you listen to them,

You won't be the fool.

You'll be well-behaved.

Your work will be done.

We'll pass o'er your house.

You can finally have fun!

So look to your tree,

And the bright Christmas lights.

And remember we're here

Lurking in the dark night.

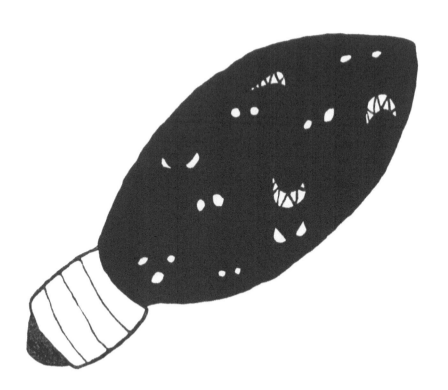

Learn more about the Yuletide Monsters

La Befana

La Befana is found throughout Italy, where she visits both nice and naughty children. On Epiphany Eve, she brings smalls gifts and treats to well-behaved children. For children who have not listened to their parents, she might leave coal, a stick, garlic, or an onion.

Some believe she is the ancient Roman goddess Strenia (the goddess of well-being and the New Year). According to Christian legend, the Three Wise Men stopped to ask La Befana for directions to baby Jesus. Another story says La Befana went to visit baby Jesus after her own baby died. Jesus decided to give the witch a gift: since she lost her child, she would be a mother to all children.

Today, La Befana looks like an ugly old lady. She rides on her broom, which she also uses to clean your house when she visits. She is covered in soot since she likes to come down your chimney. Families will leave out a glass of wine for her, but don't stay up too late! If she spots you, she might hit you with her broom before flying away!

Tomtar

The Tomtar date back to pre-Christian times in Denmark, Norway, and Sweden (also known as Scandinavia). Tomtar is the Swedish name for these creatures. Sometimes they live in a barn or somewhere in a home, and other times, they live in massive burial mounds. According to legend, the Tomtar are spirits of the first people who lived in a house.

They might look like elves or gnomes to you—they are small with a long white beard, and they like to wear bright red hats.

They may look cute, but Tomtar are very temperamental. If you respect them, they will protect your home and help with chores. But if you are rude, they like to play tricks on you. They might try to make you go crazy or even bite you.

Don't mess up what a Tomtar has cleaned. If something falls to the floor, warn them before it can hit them (since they are so small). An excellent way to make the Tomtar like you is to leave out a bowl of porridge or oatmeal on Christmas Eve with a nice big slice of butter on top.

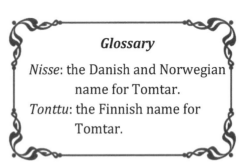

Glossary

Nisse: the Danish and Norwegian name for Tomtar.

Tonttu: the Finnish name for Tomtar.

Knecht Ruprecht

"Farmhand Rupert" or "Servant Rupert" dates back to the 1600s in German folklore. Today, he is one of St. Nicholas's companions and can be spotted in the famous Nuremberg Christmas parade. Some think he was even adopted by St. Nicholas when he was a little boy!

He likes to wear black or brown robes with a pointed hood. He carries a long staff or walking stick, bells, and a bag full of ashes. Sometimes he rides a white horse and is even accompanied by fairies.

Long ago, Knecht Ruprecht could have been a house spirit, fairy, or sprite. These creatures could be good or evil, depending on your behavior. The word *Ruprecht* was a common name for the Devil in Germany. However, with the spread of Christianity, Knecht Ruprecht has transformed from a sprite or devil into a helper today.

On St. Nicholas Day (December 6th), Knecht Ruprecht will ask children if they can pray. If the answer is yes, he will give them apples, nuts, and gingerbread. If the answer is no, he hits them with his bag of ashes and leaves a stick in their shoe for their parents to spank them if they're bad.

Frau Perchta

Frau Perchta's name means "the Bright One" in Old High German (spoken from 750-1050AD). Pre-Christianity, Perchta was an Alpine goddess of spinning and weaving, and her celebration happened to coincide with the Twelve Days of Christmas (the time between Christmas and Epiphany). When Christianity arrived in the region, the goddess was turned into a witch.

If you were respectful and obeyed Perchta, she would look beautiful to you and even leave a silver coin in your shoe. But if you angered her, she would look ugly and scary and even try to stuff you with rocks and straw!

To keep Perchta happy, many people eat her favorite meal—fish and gruel and even cake. Others like to leave her food and drink to receive a blessing in the coming year though many people were forced to stop doing this in the 1400s because the Church did not like it.

Supposedly, witches would rub goose fat all over themselves to fly faster and better. In the past, people left out a bowl of goose fat on their front steps for Frau Perchta. Some people believe this is why the traditional Christmas meal is a goose.

Karakoncolos

The Karakoncolos might be the strangest looking Yuletide monster! They were originally found in late Ottoman Turkish myths. People have described him as being a mix of a devil and a Sasquatch (or Bigfoot). He's tall and hairy and is found in places like Turkey and Bulgaria.

In Turkey, he stands on street corners, asking people riddles. If the answer includes the word "black," they are free to go. This is because the Turkish word for "black" is "kara," just like part of his name: Karakoncolos. These creatures can also change the sound of their voices to lure people into the night.

Luckily, the Karakoncolos can only come out during the first ten days of the Heart of Winter around New Years. There are many things that they don't like that you can use to protect yourself and your home such as basil and ivy, goat masks, embroidery, and even crafts. In Bulgaria, some people even dance in the street to scare away evil spirits. This tradition dates back to before Ancient Rome!

Glossary

Zemheri: The time between December 22nd and January 21st. Also known as the Heart of Winter.

Mari Lwyd

You may have heard the Christmas song, "Here we come a-wassailing among the leaves so green!" But do you know what "wassailing" is? It's similar to Christmas caroling today, where people go from door to door, singing songs. Many times, food and drink are exchanged, including wassail (a hot mulled cider dating back to Medieval times).

In Wales, there is a wassailing tradition, unlike any other, where friends decorate a horse's skull with ribbons, bells, flowers, and other decorations, and go wassailing.

People believe this is an ancient tradition with pre-Christian roots. However, it only became popular in the 1800s.

If you want to try a Mari Lwyd wassail, you need to practice your singing! You'll go from house to house and request to go inside for a snack. The homeowners will respond with their own songs. Back and forth, the singing contest will go until the homeowners give up and allow you inside for a treat and maybe even some hot apple cider.

Sack Man

There are many figures in Yuletide folklore like the Sack Man, which is why he doesn't have a specific name. He's a bogeyman that some parents use to scare their children and make them behave.

The Sack Man is most popular in Latin countries such as Spain, Portugal, Brazil, and other parts of Latin America. But he is also very popular in Haiti, Southern Europe, South Africa, Russia, and even parts of Asia such as India, Korea, and Vietnam.

Because so many different cultures have their own Sack Man, descriptions of him sometimes vary. But one thing is always the same: he is a tall man who carries a sack on his back. What is his sack for? Not presents like Santa Claus! With his sack, he takes naughty children away from their homes.

Some names he likes to go by are Tonton Macoute/Uncle Gunnysack (Haiti), Babay/бабай/Old Man (Russia), Bori Baba/Father Sack (India), Abu I Kees/كيس و اب/The Man with the Bag (Lebanon), El hombre del Saco/the Bag Man (Spanish speaking countries), and mangtae yeonggam/망태 영감/Old Man with a Sack (Korea).

Grýla, the Yule Lads, and their Yule Cat

Grýla and her wicked family have gone through several changes over the years. They haven't always been part of Icelandic Christmas celebrations, but they're more popular today than ever!

Grýla is a giantess (a girl giant) who lives in the Dimmuborgir lava fields with her husband, a troll named Leppalúði and the Yule Lads. She first appeared in a story called the *Prose Edda* by a man named Snorri Sturluson almost 1,000 years ago! However, she only became connected with Christmas in the 1600s as a way for parents to keep children from venturing outside in the dangerous Icelandic winters.

According to the stories, Grýla would watch children all year long, looking for the naughty ones. When winter arrived, she would venture into the villages and eat the disobedient children. Her favorite food is said to be a stew made from naughty children. Supposedly she is always hungry and sometimes shares her stew with her thirteen sons, known as the Yule Lads.

In the past, the Yule Lads were evil and nasty, but today they are mischievous and like to play tricks on people. When a child has been nice throughout the year, they leave a gift in their shoe... and a potato if you haven't been very good. Lucky for us, they're only allowed out of the lava fields from December 12th-January 6th.

There are thirteen Yule Lads, and they all have silly names, making them even less scary than they were hundreds of years ago.
1. Giljagaur/Gully Gawk (likes to hide in gullies)
2. Stekkjarstaur/Sheep Coat-Clod (he picks on sheep)
3. Stúfur/Stubby (he's short)
4. Þvörusleikir/Spoon-Licker (he likes to lick wooden spoons)
5. Pottaskefill/Pot-Scraper (he steals leftovers from pots)
6. Askasleikir/Bowl-Licker (he takes wooden bowls called "askur bowls")
7. Hurðaskellir/Door-Slammer (he slams doors)
8. Skyrgámur/Skyr-Gobbler (he likes to eat skyr/yogurt)
9. Bjúgnakraekir/Sausage-Swiper (he steals smoked sausages)
10. Gluggagaegir/Window-Peeper (he likes to look through windows)
11. GáttaÞefur/Doorway-Sniffer (he has a large nose that he uses to locate *laufabrauð* or leaf bread)
12. Ketkrókur/Meat-Hook (uses a hook to steal meat)
13. Kertasníkir/Candle-Stealer (he follows children to steal their candles)

The Yule Lads might make you think that these Icelandic figures aren't scary, but wait until you meet *Jólakötturinn* or the Yule Cat.

She is Grýla's pet and lurks in the snowy countryside. She is described as being black and larger than a house with shining eyes and sharp whiskers that could cut you. Some people think she is as old as Grýla, but she only appeared in stories in the 1800s.

According to legend, she roams Iceland looking for people who haven't gotten any new clothes by Christmas Eve. If you haven't gotten socks or a shirt or a hat, she'll eat you up!

These legends of Grýla eating children and the Yule Cat gobbling up anyone without a new pair of pants might seem scary to you, but they each had a very important lesson.

Winters in Iceland (especially long ago) were cold, dark, and extremely dangerous. If a child left home to play outside as the sun was setting, many times, they wouldn't return home. These stories helped to keep children safe and close to home. The stories of Grýla also helped to make sure everyone in the family got all of the work done before the long winter months so everyone could survive.

The legend of the Yule Cat has a similar meaning. The threat of a giant cat coming to get you ensured that you finished all your weaving, knitting, and sewing before winter arrived.

Belsnickel

The Belsnickel is similar to Knecht Ruprecht but is more well-known outside of Europe today. He has his origins in Germany, but he has become popular in Pennsylvania Deutsch communities in America. He can be found in Christmas celebrations in New York, Pennsylvania, and Maryland. He first appeared in the 1800s but is making a comeback today.

His name comes from the word "fur" and a nickname for Nicholas. He likes to wear furs and sometimes a mask and even antlers. He carries a stick to hit naughty children and has pockets full of sweets, cakes, and nuts for good children.

He visits homes one to two weeks before Christmas. When he knocks on the door, children must answer the door and answer a question or sing a song to get a treat.

In some versions of the story, the Belsnickel is actually a grumpy woman and not a grumpy old man.

Kallikantzaros

These little monsters look like goblins, originating in Southern European folklore. The Kallikantzaros can be found in countries like Greece, Bulgaria, Serbia, Albania, Cyprus, and Bosnia. They are usually described as looking like tiny humans, all black with long tails.

Kallikantzaros live underground and spend the whole year trying to chop down the World Tree. However, during the Twelve Days of Christmas, they are allowed to come to Earth and cause mischief. Lucky for us, by the time they return underground, the World Tree has healed itself, and they have to start all over!

The days between Christmas and Epiphany are called the "unbaptized days" when evil spirits are free to roam the Earth, including the Kallikantzaros. You can protect your house from them by burning a Yule log in the fireplace. You can also throw smelly shoes in the fire, use straw and garlic to keep them out of the house, and place a colander outside your door. Why a colander? Kallikantzaros can't count above two because three is a holy number. They spend all night trying to count the holes but have to start over every time they get to three.

> **Glossary**
>
> *Moriai*: the name of the World Tree. In Greece, the World Tree is an olive tree or a moria.

Lussi

Lussi is actually two people in one: the beautiful St. Lucia and the scary Lussi. In Norway and Sweden, December 13th is St. Lucia's Day. It was originally the celebration of the Winter Solstice and has survived since the Middle Ages. To many, St. Lucia's Day has always belonged to the rich and powerful while Lussi's Long Night belonged to the country folk and poor.

Lussi Langnatte or Lussi's Long Night is the night before St. Lucia's Day and was taken very seriously by everyone. It was believed that monsters and ghosts would join Lussi as she flew on her broom. They would destroy crops and homes and kidnap anyone not safe in their beds.

To protect yourself from Lussi, all of your work needed to be done (such as harvesting food, cleaning the house, and spinning wool). If you didn't complete your chores, Lussi would smash your chimney and come down to scare you.

There were other ways to keep Lussi away, including burning fires, carving the name "Lussi" on doors, fences, and walls, and even hanging axes, knives, and scissors over doorways. And you should never forget to leave out Lussi's favorite treat: a saffron bun.

Glossary

Oskorei: demons and trolls on the Wild Hunt.

Lussevaka: a person who stays up all night to keep the fire going.

Krampus

Perhaps the most famous Yuletide Monster of them all, Krampus has been around for thousands of years, long before Christmas and Christianity. He is described as a goat-like demon, with horns, a long tongue, black and hairy with chains, sticks, and a basket to carry naughty children to the Underworld.

He's most famously found in Austria, a part of Germany called Bavaria, Croatia, Hungary, and Northern Italy. At first, it didn't seem like this demon would survive the spread of Christianity, but he was so popular, they turned him into a Christmas demon who works with St. Nicholas. Today, St. Nicholas or Santa Claus rewards good children, and Krampus punishes naughty children.

Krampusnacht is celebrated every year on the night before St. Nicholas Day on December 5th. On this night, Krampus roams the streets, visiting the homes of children who have misbehaved over the last year. In some cities, there is a *Krampuslauf* or a Krampus Run where people dress up as Krampus, hold a parade and a bonfire, and celebrate the darker side of wintertime.

> ### Glossary
>
> *Ruten:* a bundle of birch twigs used to punish naughty children.
>
> *Krampusnacht:* Krampus Night, the night before St. Nicholas Day.

About the Author

Writer, anthropologist, and former international English teacher, Amanda R. Woomer, has been fascinated by all things that go bump in the night since she was a little girl. She won her first prize for her writing when she was only 12 years old, and today, she is the owner of Spook-Eats and a writer for the award-winning *Haunted Magazine*. She is the author of several books for adults as well as book one in Creepy Books for Creepy Kids: *The Cryptid ABC Book.* Follow her spooky adventures at spookeats.com.

Made in United States
Troutdale, OR
11/11/2024

24658577R00071